This one's for my mom,
NELL ORUM STOLL-JONES

Once there were three white mice
on a piece of white paper.

Mouse Paint

Ellen Stoll Walsh

ORCHARD BOOKS

LONDON

ORCHARD BOOKS
96 Leonard Street, London EC2A 4RH
Orchard Books Australia
14 Mars Road, Lane Cove, NSW 2066
Copyright © Ellen Stoll Walsh 1989
Originally published in the United States in 1989 by Harcourt Brace Jovanovich, Publishers
First published in Great Britain 1989
First paperback publication 1991
A CIP catalogue record for this book is available from
the British Library.
1 85213 179 9 (hardback)
1 85213 320 1 (paperback)
Printed in Belgium

The cat couldn't find them.

One day, while the cat was asleep,
the mice saw three jars of paint —

one red, one yellow, and one blue.

They thought it was Mouse Paint.
They climbed right in.

Then one was red, one was yellow,
and one was blue.

They dripped puddles of paint
onto the paper.

The puddles looked like fun.

The red mouse stepped into
a yellow puddle and did a little dance.

His red feet stirred
the yellow puddle until . . .

"Look," he cried.

"Red feet in a yellow puddle
make orange!"

The yellow mouse hopped
into a blue puddle.

His feet mixed and stirred
and stirred and mixed until . . .

"Look down," said the red mouse
and the blue mouse.

"Yellow feet in a blue puddle
make green."

Then the blue mouse jumped into a red puddle.

He splashed and mixed
and danced until ...

"Purple!" they all shouted.

''Blue feet in a red puddle
make purple!''

But the paint on their fur
got sticky and stiff.

So they washed themselves down
to a nice soft white

and painted the paper instead.
They painted one part red

and one part yellow

and one part blue.

They mixed red and yellow
to paint an orange part,

yellow and blue to paint a green part,

and blue and red to paint a purple part.

But they left some white
because of the cat.